Maxwell the Monkey Barber

by Cale Atkinson

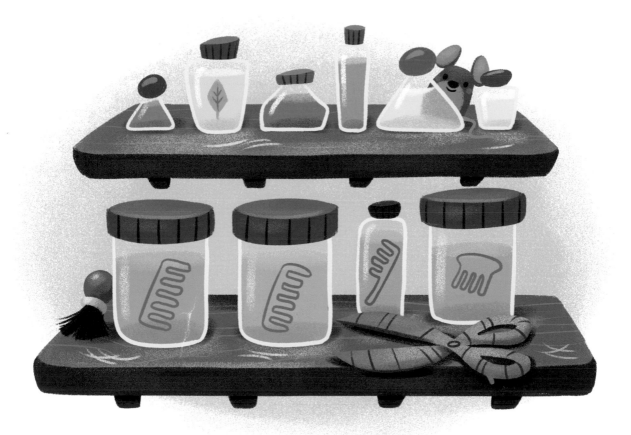

Owlkids Books

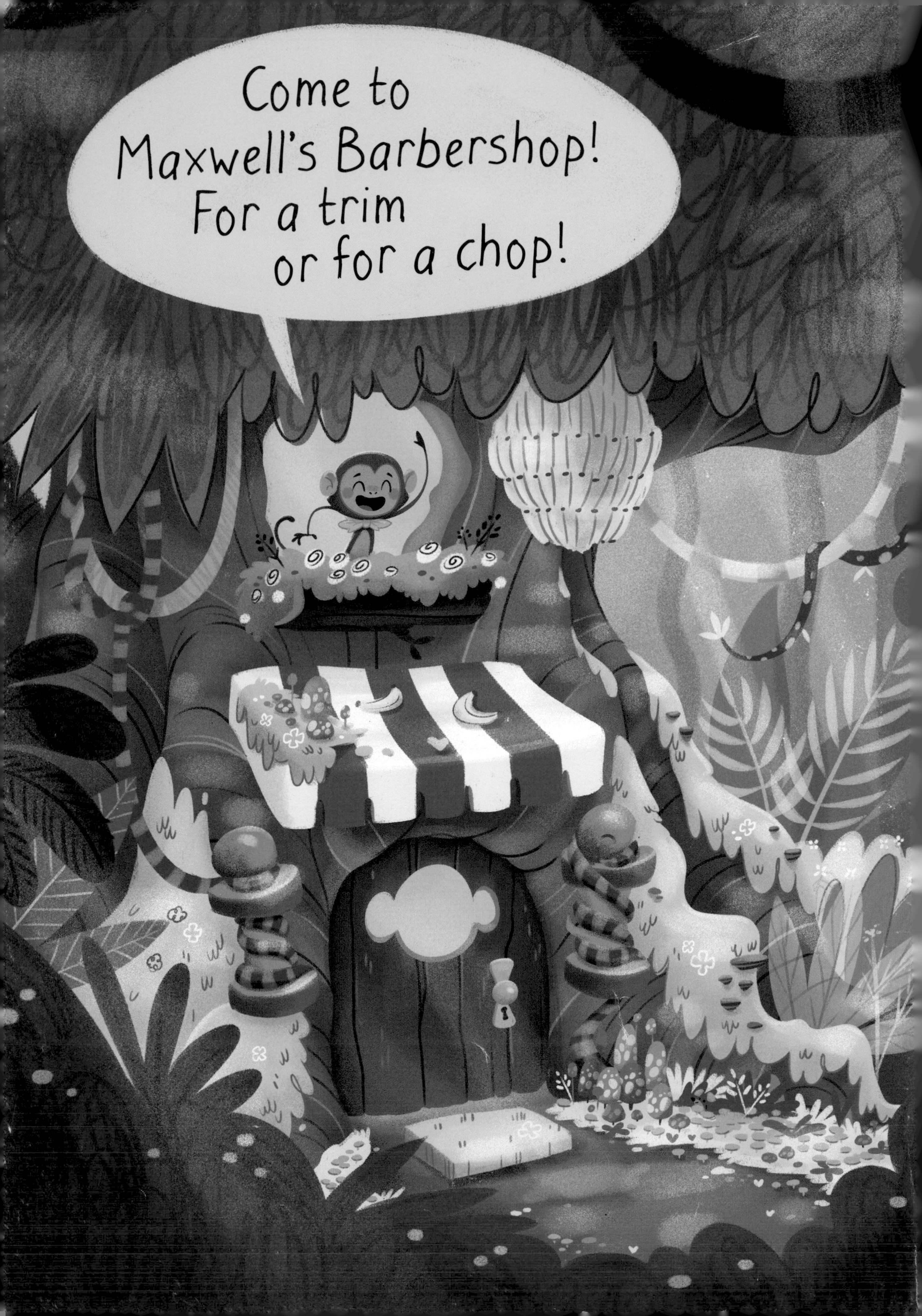
Come to Maxwell's Barbershop! For a trim or for a chop!

He grabbed his scissors
and lowered the chair,
ready at nine to cut some hair.

Baboon swung in
with curls grown high.

A cut to free
what lives
inside?

After many snips
it's less a home

and more a place to run a comb.

And before you go,
might I say,
Your hair's
the best
I've seen today!

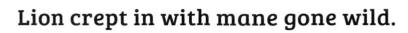

Lion crept in with mane gone wild.

Please clip
this beast to
show my style.

That beastly mane has said good-bye.
It's now so sharp it needs a tie.

And before you go,
might I say,

Your hair's
the best
I've seen today!

Bear lumbered in
with a big furry frown.

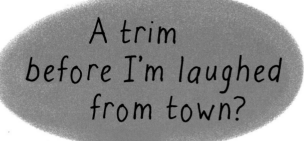

The fur is gone within a flash.

I even trimmed your long mustache.

And before you go,
might I say,

Your hair's
the best
I've seen today!

Elephant slumped in,
sad and down:

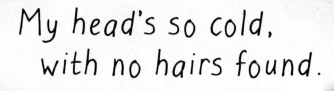

Maxwell looked and found it true —
there were no hairs,
not one,
not two.

Come back tomorrow
right at three.
I'll think of something,
just wait and see.

What was Maxwell going to do?

He thought,

he thought,

and then ... he knew!

Elephant came back, as Maxwell said,
and waiting right there for his head:
Something fine, crafted with care ...

And before you go,
might I say,
Your hair's
the best
I've seen today!

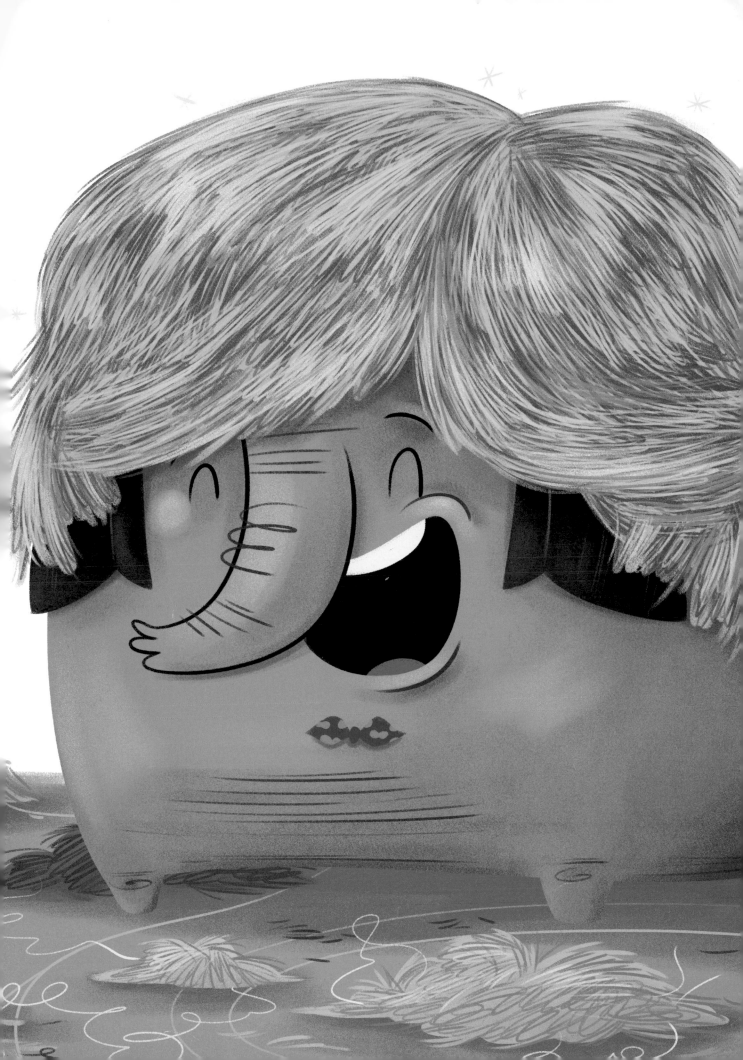

Everyone heard of elephant's new 'do,
and hair or no hair,
they wanted one, too!

Come one, come all,
to Maxwell's shop!

For a wig or for a chop!

Dedicated to all the wild beasts
out there with one hair too many
or one hair too few.
~ Cale

Text and illustrations © 2016 Cale Atkinson

Owlkids Books acknowledges the financial support of the Canada Council for the Arts, the Ontario Arts
Council, the Government of Canada through the Canada Book Fund (CBF) and the Government of Ontario
through the Ontario Media Development Corporation's Book Initiative for our publishing activities.

Published in Canada by Published in the United States by
Owlkids Books Inc. Owlkids Books Inc.
10 Lower Spadina Avenue 1700 Fourth Street
Toronto, ON M5V 2Z2 Berkeley, CA 94710

Library and Archives Canada Cataloguing in Publication

Atkinson, Cale, author, illustrator
    Maxwell the monkey barber / Cale Atkinson.

ISBN: 978-1-77147-103-9

    I. Title.

PS8601.T547M39 2016   jC813'.6   C2015-907768-0

Library of Congress Control Number: 2015956792

Edited by: Jessica Burgess
Designed by: Barb Kelly

  **ONTARIO ARTS COUNCIL** **CONSEIL DES ARTS DE L'ONTARIO** an Ontario government agency un organisme du gouvernement de l'Ontario   **Canada Council for the Arts**   **Conseil des Arts du Canada**   **Canadä**

Manufactured in Shenzhen, China, in March 2016,
by C&C Joint Printing Co.
Job #HP6227

A   B   C   D   E   F

 Owl kids Publisher of Chirp, chickaDEE and OWL
www.owlkidsbooks.com | Owlkids Books is a division of  **Bayard** CANADA